Night of the Veggie Monster

GEORGE McCLEMENTS

BLOOMSBURY
CHILDREN'S
BOOKS

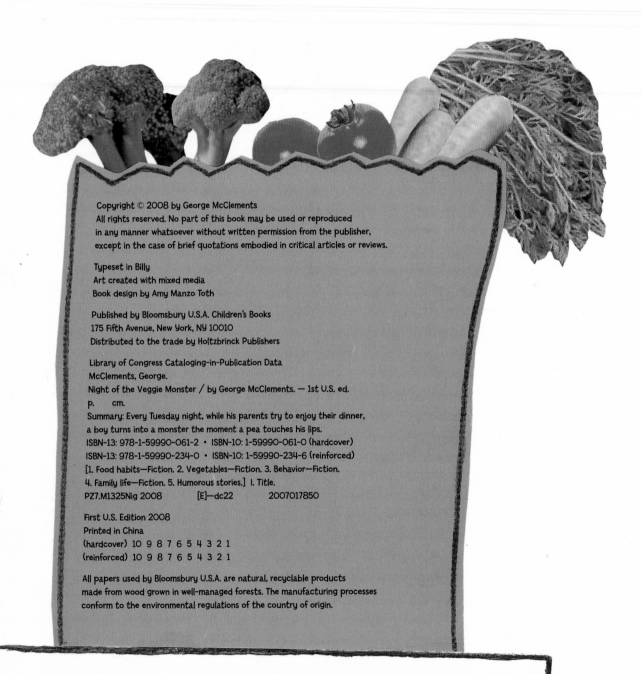

Typeset in Billy
Art created with mixed media
Book design by Amy Manzo Toth

Published by Bloomsbury U.S.A. Children's Books
175 Fifth Avenue, New York, NY 10010
Distributed to the trade by Holtzbrinck Publishers

Library of Congress Cataloging-in-Publication Data
McClements, George.
Night of the Veggie Monster / by George McClements. — 1st U.S. ed.
p.   cm.
Summary: Every Tuesday night, while his parents try to enjoy their dinner,
a boy turns into a monster the moment a pea touches his lips.
ISBN-13: 978-1-59990-061-2 • ISBN-10: 1-59990-061-0 (hardcover)
ISBN-13: 978-1-59990-234-0 • ISBN-10: 1-59990-234-6 (reinforced)
[1. Food habits—Fiction. 2. Vegetables—Fiction. 3. Behavior—Fiction.
4. Family life—Fiction. 5. Humorous stories.] I. Title.
PZ7.M1325Nig 2008   [E]—dc22   2007017850

First U.S. Edition 2008
Printed in China
(hardcover) 10 9 8 7 6 5 4 3 2 1
(reinforced) 10 9 8 7 6 5 4 3 2 1

All papers used by Bloomsbury U.S.A. are natural, recyclable products
made from wood grown in well-managed forests. The manufacturing processes
conform to the environmental regulations of the country of origin.

Green Is Good

Finicky Eaters

Vegetables 4 Kids

For my sweet peas:

Rachel, Samuel, and Matthew

Something **TERRIBLE** happens every Tuesday night.

PEAS!

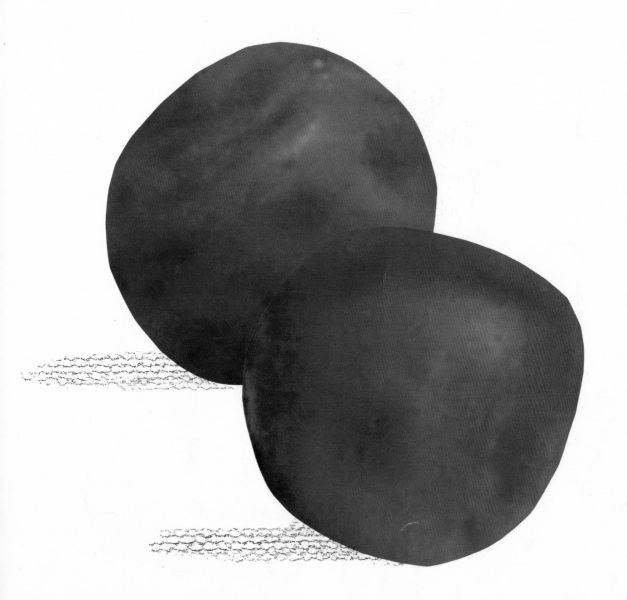

They have no idea what **one tiny** pea does to me.

With just the
slightest
touch . . .

. . . it begins.

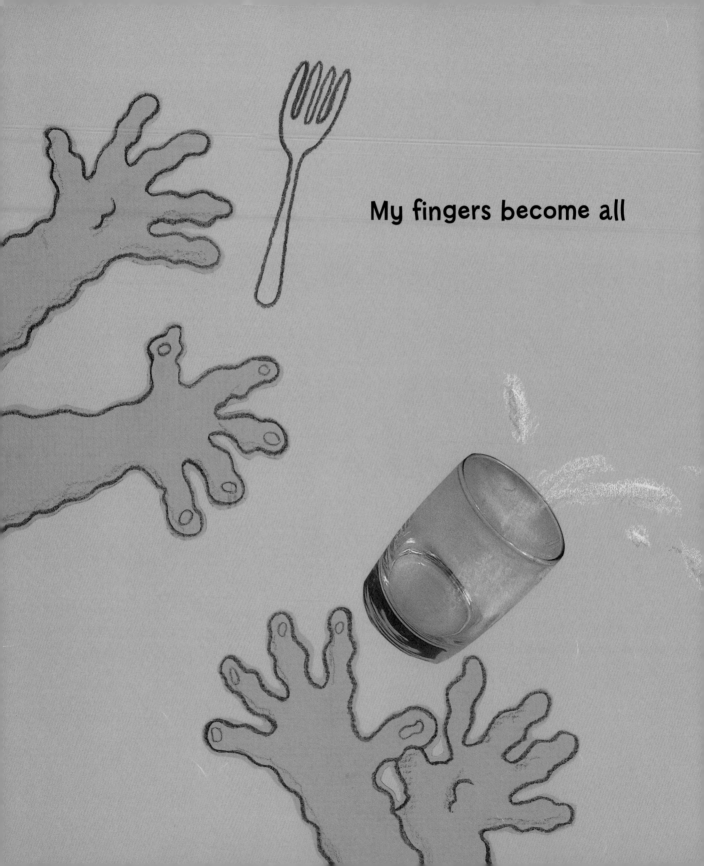

My fingers become all

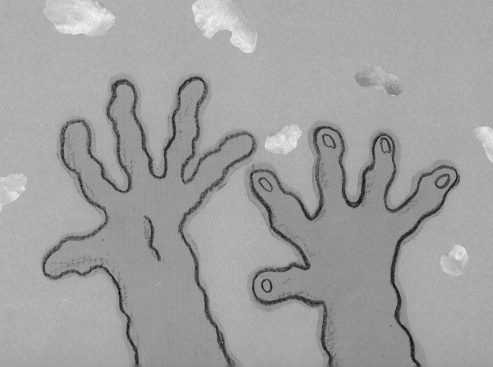

As the pea rests in my mouth,

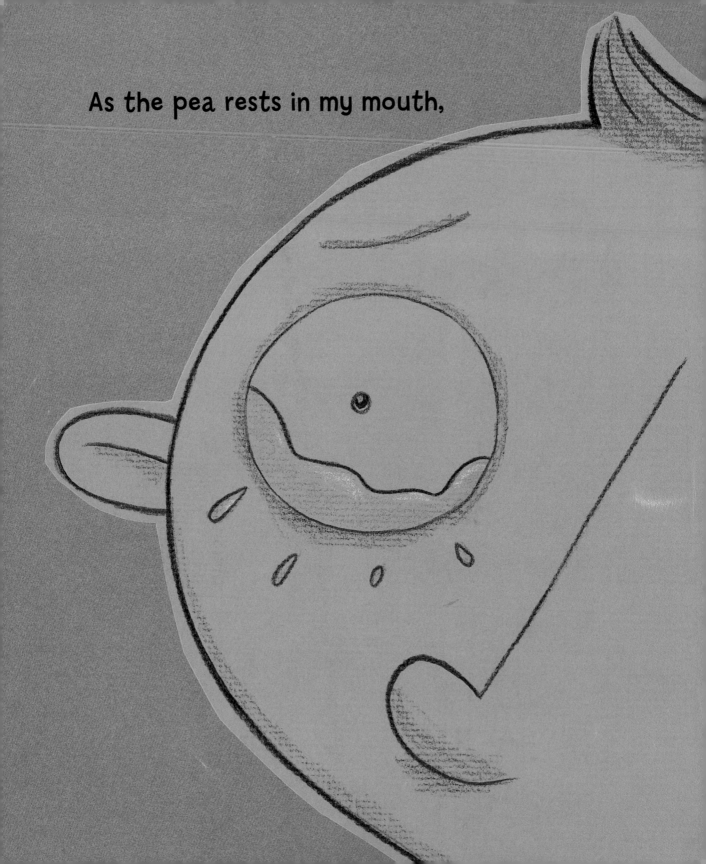

My toes
TWIST and
CURL UP
in my shoes.

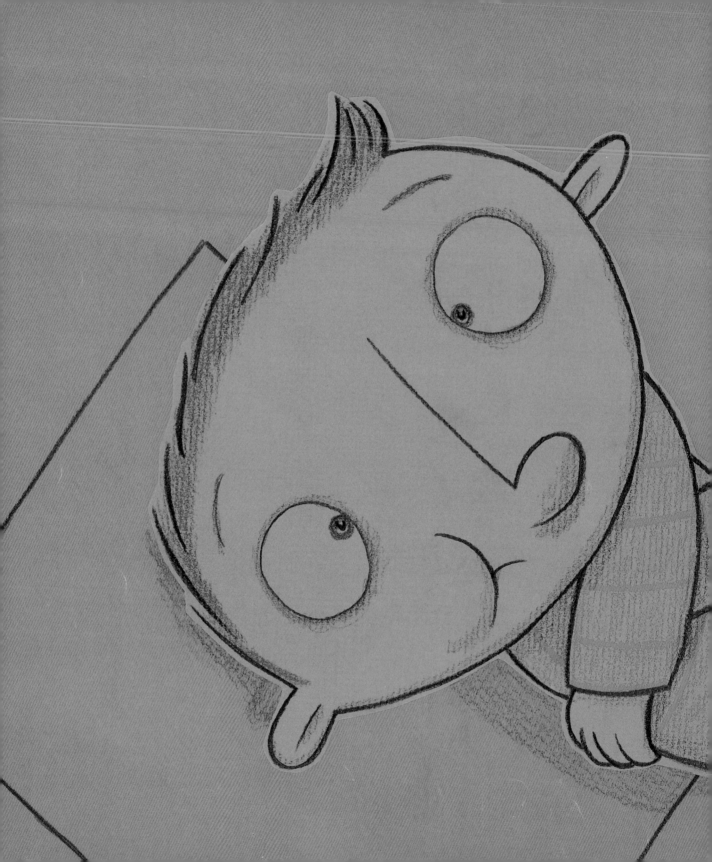

I **SQUIRM** in my seat. I try to keep control but the **pea** is too strong. I start to transform into...

. . . a **VEGGIE MONSTER!**

Ready to **Smash** the chairs!
Ready to *tip* the table!
Ready to . . .

. . . GULP!

I swallowed the pea.

I actually swallowed the pea.

It tasted all right, really.

Well, I guess peas are okay.
But there is still a danger!

Because **tomorrow** is WEDNESDAY,
and on **WEDNESDAY** we have . . .